LEAVING AREA 51

A NOVELLETTE

L. P. HAWK

This is a work of fiction. Names, characters, places, brands, media, and incidents are either the product of the author's imagination or are used fictitiously. Any resemblance to similarly named places or to persons living or deceased is unintentional.

ACKNOWLEDGMENTS

First and foremost, I have my brothers to thank for my fascination with UFOs and all things otherworldly—

Bruce, who shares my interest in Giorgio Tsoukalos and his *Ancient Aliens*, and George Noory's *Coast to Coast* radio show,

Doug, who started it all by telling his kid sister about the UFO he saw in New Mexico during his college days,

And Gary, who was my TV buddy when we watched that 1970s show *Project UFO*. I always hoped we'd see one of our own.

And most of all, I give praise and glory to my Lord and Savior Jesus Christ, who reminded me as I wrote this story that He alone is that "something more" I keep seeking.

To my boys, Wesley and Wayde. Always keep looking up. Always keep seeking.

"THERE'S ORION," NICKELETTE said, leaning over the deck railing to point toward the southeast. "I see Orion."

Buck snorted as he continued scanning the skies directly above. "Nickelette, you say that literally every time we're out here. We all know you can find Orion."

Nickelette turned to glare at her brother in the darkness. "Well, excuse me. I happen to like Orion. He's my favorite constellation."

"Maybe he likes you too," Buck retorted with a saucy grin. "You may actually get a date for prom."

"Oh, shut up, Buck."

"No, you shut up, Nickelette."

"Why don't you both shut up?" Bill lowered his binoculars long enough to look sharply at both of them. "It's a good thing meteorites can't hear, or the two of you would scare them off."

"Dad, they're not meteor*ites*; they're just meteors," Buck said. "They're only meteor*ites* if they hit the ground. Shooting stars don't hit the ground."

"How do you know whether they hit the ground or not?" Bill laid the binoculars on the table and crossed his arms, unwilling to admit his error.

"Seriously, Dad?" Nickelette rolled her eyes. "If a meteorite hit the ground, you'd hear it, and you'd see the explosion."

Penny sat in the far corner of the deck, staring up at the sky and half-listening to the combination banter and science lesson going on right next to her. She had heard the same taunts and squabbles many times before. Wintertime stargazing had been a Dimeler family tradition since Buck and Nickelette were old enough to recognize the constellations in the sky. Since the kids were now teenagers and often out and about with friends, and since Bill had recently received a long-desired promotion at work that had increased his hours, these family nights were becoming more and more rare. She was determined to treasure every moment.

As they all went back to watching the sky, flashing red and white lights caught Penny's eye. She turned to watch a jet moving quickly from east to west. Moments later, a second jet came past going in the opposite direction, much lower in the sky as it approached the airport in Harrisburg. Stargazing was forgotten for Penny as she turned her attention to the numerous passing planes and helicopters. She let out a wistful sigh. *So many planes*, she said to herself. *Who's on those planes, and where are they going?*

She rose from her chair to lean against the chimney. One of the jets disappeared beyond the mountain, and she rested her head against the cold stone, staring at the spot where the lights had vanished as though willing the jet to return for her. She had seldom been more than a day's drive away from Dillsburg, where she'd grown up, married, and raised her family.

Sometimes when her friends or relatives talked about their travels to some island paradise or shared pictures of their Disney vacations, Penny entertained the slightest twinge of envious wanderlust, but it usually passed quickly. However, on nights like these, when the sky above seemed to go on forever, and her home seemed more stifling than cozy, she watched the planes go by and just wished—

"Dad, look! What's that?" Buck was looking straight up and pointing at something. "There's a really faint light up there, moving fast."

Bill got to his feet, as though doing so would bridge some of the distance between himself and whatever point of interest his son had discovered. He squinted and cupped his hands around his eyes, and then reached for his binoculars. "Where is it? What am I supposed to be looking at?"

"It's right up there," Buck said, stumbling against a chair as he hurried to his father's side. He leaned close and pointed again. "It's just now passing that bright star."

"Oh! I see it," Penny said, excited. "What is it? It's too high up to be a jet."

"I see it too!" Nickelette let out a little squeak. "Maybe it's a UFO; maybe it'll land."

"Get real," Buck hooted. "Aliens wouldn't come within a million miles of *Dulls*burg."

"You kids," Bill said with disdain. "There's no such thing as UFOs or aliens."

A slight chill raced down Penny's spine as she shot her husband a sidelong glance. While her daughter was currently enthralled by UFOs and aliens, and was quite certain they existed, she herself was on the fence about extraterrestrials, but truth be told, she really wanted there to be something else out there. "Well then, what is it?"

"It's probably a satellite," he responded matter-of-factly. "There are more than three thousand of those things orbiting the earth."

"Three *thousand*?" Nickelette gaped at her father.

"Absolutely." Bill raised his binoculars to his eyes again, following the satellite as it disappeared into the distance. "Weather satellites and communication satellites—"

"And don't forget the spy satellites," Buck interrupted, returning to his chair. "The Russians are watching us."

"Why would the Russians want to watch Dillsburg?" Nickelette asked, propping her feet up on the table to rock her chair. "Or *Dulls*burg, as you like calling it."

"Not Dillsburg, dorko. The United States."

Penny shook her head as her children began squabbling once more. As she turned her attention back to the skies, she found herself wishing her family would go inside so she could scan the sky in peace and be alone with her thoughts.

A short time later, Bill slid the binoculars back into their leather case and got to his feet. "Well, I think I'm done. It's getting too cold for me. You kids coming?"

Nickelette looked up from her phone. Her face, illuminated by the bright screen, appeared almost alien-like. "I'm done too." She got up quickly and started toward the door, likely heading for her bedroom where she would continue texting her friends or scrolling her social media accounts as she did every night.

Buck stood up and started after her. "It's dead out here tonight. Not one single meteor."

Nickelette glanced over her shoulder and laughed. "I guess Dullsburg is even too dull for meteors."

The kids disappeared inside, and Bill went to the door. Seeing that Penny hadn't moved from her spot, he turned to her and asked, "You coming, Pen?"

"Not just yet." She wrapped her coat more tightly around her and shoved her hands into her pockets. "It's a nice night; I'll be in shortly."

"Suit yourself." Bill went inside and shut the door against the cold.

Finally alone, Penny let out a happy sigh and tipped her head back to stare up at the sky. She loved stargazing on clear, cold winter nights. There wasn't a hint of haze or humidity in the air, and the stars glimmered like jewels, some appearing to be close enough to touch. Scanning the sky, she silently greeted

Orion and acknowledged his dogs Canis Major and Minor, then found Cassiopeia and the Big and Little Dippers.

Several more planes went by, followed by what appeared to be a police helicopter traveling fast over the ridge near her house. As her eyes skimmed the western horizon, another bright light caught her eye. Thinking it was another jet coming in to land at Harrisburg, she fixed her gaze upon it, letting her mind wander. *Where are the people coming from,* she wondered again, *and what adventure are they on their way to?*

A mantle of melancholy settled over her once more as she compared the grand journeys of the airborne travelers with her own mundane life. She had always wanted to travel, to experience some of the exciting places her friends and family had, but it seemed that every time an opportunity presented itself, the time wasn't right, or the money wasn't there, or she simply couldn't muster up the courage to go. She had spent much of her adult life caring for both her and Bill's aging parents and her own children, and as a result, she hadn't made time for adventures of her own. She didn't regret the time and energy invested in caring for others; it was just that sometimes, she longed for…more.

Lost in her thoughts, Penny didn't realize that the light had continued to come closer and closer, and get brighter and brighter, until its hue changed from white to pink to blue and then back to white. *I don't think that's a plane. What is it?* As she stared at the light, mesmerized, a door, long shut and forgotten, opened in her mind. Something similar had happened before, many years ago, when she was a child.

Penny hadn't been able to sleep. Her parents had argued for hours in the living room right after her mother had tucked her in, and finally Daddy had stormed out, slamming the door behind him. She had sat at her bedroom window ever since, watching the dark street for Daddy's car to return. This scenario had played out many times over the past few months, and each time it seemed Daddy stayed away longer. Sometimes she wished she could run away, away from the fighting, away from Daddy's absences, away from Mommy's sullen tolerance of their way of life. But she couldn't. Where would she go?

While she kept her vigil, a bright light appeared above the horizon. As she watched, it grew brighter and brighter as it came closer and closer, until it was almost right on top of the house. Without warning, a silver-blue beam of light extended from the parent light, enveloping her. Suddenly, she found herself above the house, floating in the beam of light. She knew she should be frightened, but she wasn't. She was more curious.

A gentle voice spoke to her, not out loud, but inside her head. "Penny...Penny, come with us. Are you coming? Penny...Penny..."

Penny blinked hard several times, and she reached out to grip the edge of the table as she was yanked from her ruminations. To her surprise, the bright light was still there, directly overhead now, and a silver-blue beam enveloped her. Even more surprising, she could still hear the voice, except now she heard it aloud, from somewhere close by.

"Penny? Are you coming inside, or are you spending the night out there?"

She suddenly recognized the voice as Bill's. He and the kids had gone inside long ago—how long ago, exactly?—and he wanted her to come inside too. She glanced up at the bright light, somehow knowing that it, too, wanted her to come inside, not inside the house, but inside whatever craft was hidden within the bright light. Part of her wanted to go with them, but a bigger part of her was afraid. *Where would they take me? What would happen to Bill and the kids?*

Even as the doubts took form in her mind, the silver-blue beam vanished, and the bright light shot across the sky, disappearing in an instant.

"Did you see that?" Bill burst through the back door, staring wide-eyed as he pointed skyward. "Did you see that meteorite? It was huge! A fireball!"

A meteorite? Was that what it had been? She looked at Bill and then back to the inky midnight sky. "No, I...I didn't see anything. I must have dozed off."

Hours later, Penny lay awake, neither lulled nor disturbed by the hum of the white noise machine and the steady buzz saw of Bill's snoring. She stared at the dim outline of the overhead light and replayed her earlier experience over and over again in her mind. She knew she hadn't imagined the light because Bill had seen it too, although he had interpreted it as a meteorite, a fireball. But it hadn't been a meteor...had it? She wasn't a scientist, but even she knew meteors didn't act the way that light had acted.

Penny rolled onto her side to stare at the dim, curtained, square window on her side of the room, allowing her thoughts to wander back to the dark, painful days of her parents' separation and subsequent divorce. She had seen the mysterious light, sensed the telepathic invitation, and found herself floating above the house two more times before she told Aunt Tianna, who then told Penny's mother, who promptly took Penny to a counselor, fearing that the strain of the divorce had become too much for her. Thankfully, Dr. Rahn hadn't been overly concerned about Penny's *imaginings*, as he'd called them. He'd simply attributed them to a desire to travel to a fantasy world to escape her troubles and deal with her feelings of isolation and abandonment.

Letting out a sigh, Penny gently lifted the covers

and eased herself out of bed so she wouldn't wake her husband. She tiptoed over to the window and nudged the curtain aside to lean on the sill and peer out. The neighborhood was quiet and dark, and the only lights in the sky now were the stars and one lone jet racing past to the east. *What if Dr. Rahn was right?* she mused. *What if I did imagine that light back then? But if I did imagine it because I was unhappy and wanted to escape*—she turned to gaze in the direction of her sleeping husband—*then why did I see it tonight?*

"I just don't know what's wrong with me." Penny stirred another creamer into her coffee, staring at the swirling clouds as though she expected to see the meaning of life displayed there. "I'm not unhappy, but I'm not really happy either. As Nickelette would say, I'm stuck in an everlasting state of *meh*."

Sasha threw her head back and let out a cackle that made heads turn toward them curiously. "An everlasting state of meh. That's classic; I'll have to remember that one." She composed herself and rested a serious gaze on Penny. "But seriously, girlfriend, are you okay? Are you and Bill having problems?"

"No." She was quick to reassure her friend. "No more than usual, anyway. We just don't seem to talk or spend much time together since his promotion. I guess maybe I'm feeling a little lonely and forgotten."

Sasha nodded understandingly as she finished off her gingerbread muffin. "Yeah, no lie. It was the same with Elias after he moved up to supervisor of his shift. When Bill's more comfortable with his new responsibilities and doesn't feel like he has to prove himself anymore, things will get better."

"I suppose so." She wasn't entirely convinced that his distance was merely a matter of stress over his new position at work. She doubted it was anything as serious as an affair; she simply sensed that they were drifting apart, that after the kids graduated and moved on, they'd find they had little in common anymore. The thought scared her.

Sasha reached over to lay a hand on Penny's. "Honey, if you think things aren't right between you two, then you need to say something. The unhappiness won't go away by ignoring the problem that's causing it."

"I know that." Penny withdrew her hand and cradled her mug. "But it's more than just Bill. It's just…I don't even know what it is."

Sasha chuckled knowingly. "You know, if you were a man, people would say you were having a midlife crisis. They'd tell you to go out and buy a fancy sports car or a yacht."

"No. Just no." Penny shook her head decisively. "If I did that, there would definitely be trouble between me and Bill."

"Well, maybe it's time for you to go back to work,

you know, meet some new people, find yourself again." Sasha raised an eyebrow at her friend. "Buck and Nickelette don't need you at home all the time anymore, and it'll be good for you to get out of the house on a regular basis."

Penny felt her eyes widen apprehensively. That, at least, was good advice, she knew, but she wasn't sure she was ready for such a disruption in her routine. When Buck had started fifth grade, she had toyed with the idea of getting a part-time job and maybe taking some classes at the local community college, but Bill had insisted she stay home with the kids just a little longer, convincing her that there would be plenty of time to explore her options later. That *just a little longer* had turned into six years, and now Penny was afraid that her job skills had become obsolete, and she no longer had the desire or the courage to return to school. No, she couldn't think about getting a job. Not yet, anyway. "I'll think about it," she said noncommittally.

Sasha let out a sigh, understanding the reason behind Penny's anxiety. "Okay, so it doesn't have to be something as drastic as getting a job or buying a Maserati. Go out and get yourself a new outfit, a new piece of jewelry—with Bill's pay raise, you can afford that without draining the kids' college savings." She gestured to Penny's hair. "Or get a haircut. Girl, you've been wearing your hair the same way for as long as I've known you. Try some sleek new style or some color." She chuckled suggestively. "That'll put some spice back in your marriage, at least."

Penny smiled at her friend. She did have some options for small changes, although she doubted any of them would bring about a lasting improvement in her mood. "You're right, Sasha. Maybe I do just need a change, shake things up a little."

"That's my girl." Sasha returned her friend's smile and then flagged down the server. "Now that the counseling session is over, I'm going to shake things up and order one of those Belgian waffles."

Over the days that followed, Penny did her best to make good on her promise to make some changes in her life. She spent hours on Pinterest looking at hairstyles and haircuts, and she even pinned a dozen or so to a board she titled "The New Me," but she couldn't bring herself to do anything beyond her usual half-inch trim. She went to the mall twice in one week, once by herself and once with Nickelette, but she didn't buy anything for herself either time. She just couldn't justify spending the money on new clothes when she hardly left the house. Nickelette, however, had no such dilemma; she was treated to several new outfits and a pair of lace-up boots. Penny even managed to sneak a peek at the want-ads one morning before Bill took the paper to work. She felt more relief than she was comfortable admitting when she found nothing that appealed to her.

In the end, she remained the same Penny Dimeler she'd always been, not happy but not unhappy, merely existing, yet unable or unwilling to break out of her routine and do something different. But then one icy evening at the end of January, inspiration struck during dinner.

"Well, Penny," Bill said, mashing up his baked potato, "what do you want for your birthday this year?"

Penny stopped chewing and gave her husband a wide-eyed stare, surprised to realize that her birthday was only a little more than a month away. For as long as she could remember, she had always declared that she didn't want much—a chocolate cake from the Giant bakery, maybe a new set of pajamas or slippers, but definitely no fuss. She opened her mouth to repeat the same words she said every year, but then stopped. This year, she decided, she wanted to shake things up. This year, she wanted something different, something exciting. Laying her fork down, she said, "You know, I think this year I want to have a party."

All sounds of eating stopped as three sets of eyes snapped up to stare at her in disbelief. "What did you say?" Bill asked, leaning toward her as though he hadn't heard her.

"I said I want a party," Penny replied, more uncertainly.

"What kind of party?" Buck's expression of disbelief matched his father's.

The corners of Penny's mouth curled up in

amusement. "Why, a birthday party, of course."

"Well, of course a birthday party," Bill said in exasperation, turning his attention back to his steak as though dismissing the idea. "But why? Why this year? If it was a party you wanted, you should have said something last year, when you turned fifty. Doesn't make sense to have one this year. No one has a party for their fifty-first birthday."

Penny's initial excitement began to deflate as she realized that Bill's logic made sense. Still, she was unwilling to completely let the idea go. "I…just didn't think about it last year. I've never had a birthday party, and I just…I want one. I want something…different."

"Who would you invite?" A drop of steak sauce flew from Bill's mouth as he spoke. "Where would you have it? We don't have room here for a big party."

"Please, Dad," Buck snorted. "Mom doesn't have that many friends."

With a pang of hurt, Penny realized her son was right. "Well, it doesn't have to be a *big* party." Her voice sounded small and defeated. "I'd invite my brothers and your sister and her husband, Sasha and Elias, maybe a few people from church…" She quickly ran out of names. Turning her eyes to Buck and Nickelette, she had a sudden inspiration. "You two could invite some friends, and Bill, why don't you invite those men from the office that you always have lunch with? We could reserve the church social hall, so we wouldn't have any fuss here at the house."

Bill and Buck seemed less than enthusiastic over the suggestion, but Nickelette's eyes immediately widened with excitement. "Oh, Mom! *Could we?* That would be so cool! Oh, and I've already got the perfect theme—" she held up her hands to emphasize what she was about to say—"UFOs."

Buck slapped his hands down on the table. "Nickelette, could you give it up with the UFOs already?"

"No, listen." She refused to be dissuaded. "Not just UFOs. Mom's going to be fifty-one; we could make it a whole Area 51 theme—Keep Out signs outside, black lights and neon decorations, aliens, rockets—"

Buck's skepticism did a complete one-eighty. "Hey! That might actually work! Kenny and I could wear our black suits and sunglasses and be the Men in Black."

"Yes!" Nickelette clapped her hands, laughing.

Bill let his fork fall onto his plate. "I can't believe what I'm hearing. You kids are as bad as your mother."

"Come on, Dad. It's perfect." Buck was now completely on board with the idea. "Look at it this way; Area 51 is like a metaphor for Mom's social life. She keeps herself hidden away and only lets a handful of people in, so it's perfect."

After a moment, Bill barked out a laugh. "He's got you pegged, Penny. That's you to a T." He picked up his fork and began eating again. "So is it settled? Are we having an Area 51 party?"

Penny felt a pang of hurt over her family's

remarks. Was that really how they saw her? Reclusive? Someone who shut people out? She wanted to take back her request for a party, but would doing so merely confirm Buck's observation? Not wanting to let on that her family's jabs had upset her, she simply reached for the steak sauce and gave her children a warm smile. "I think it sounds like fun. I'll make arrangements with the church to reserve the social hall and invite a few friends, and you two can take care of the rest of the planning."

As Penny turned her attention back to her supper, Bill, Buck, and Nickelette stared at her, their mouths agape at the realization that their usually-solitary wife and mother had not only expressed the desire to have a birthday party, but had also uncharacteristically agreed to a whimsical theme.

Immediately the next day, Penny called the church office to reserve the social hall for the first Saturday of March. Much to her consternation, the church secretary was flummoxed by her request. "I...am speaking to Penny Dimeler, correct?"

"Yes, Betty, of course this is Penny Dimeler. Why would you ask such a thing?"

Betty laughed, making light of her confusion. "I'm sorry, Penny. You and Bill are usually the first ones to duck out of fellowship hour after Sunday services, so it just caught me off guard saying 'Penny Dimeler' and 'birthday party' in the same sentence. For a minute there, I had visions of aliens taking over your body…"

"Funny you should mention aliens," Penny said drily, trying to ignore the shiver that raced down her spine. "Nickelette immediately took over the planning, and she's got an Area 51 theme in mind."

"Area 51?"

"I'm turning fifty-one this year," Penny explained. "Besides, you know her fascination with all things UFO."

The light bulb came on. "Oh, so the party is Nickelette's idea. Now it makes sense."

No, it wasn't Nickelette's idea to have a party; it was mine. Before she could open her mouth to speak, Betty broke in again.

"Okay, Penny. The calendar is pretty sparse right now, so your request is no problem. I've got you plugged in for Saturday, March 7th, from 5-8 PM." A few more taps on the computer keyboard in the background. "Did you need anything else?"

"No." Anxiety began creeping in as the plan was set into motion. "I think that's everything."

"Okay then, you're all set. I'll have the form for you to sign on Sunday."

"Thank you, Betty. I'll look you up then."

As Penny ended the call, she immediately began second-guessing her decision. She had to fight the urge to call Betty back and cancel the reservation, to say she'd changed her mind. But she knew she couldn't do that. For one thing, Nickelette had her heart set on planning

this party—she didn't want to disappoint her daughter—
and for another, she didn't want to endure the I-told-
you-so attitudes of Bill and Buck if she chose to withdraw
into her own self-imposed Area 51.

In the end, she laid the phone on the counter and
left the room to find some chore to occupy her mind.

Once the party date was confirmed, planning
immediately commenced. Penny drew up her guest list,
and Buck designed and printed out a stack of Area 51-
themed invitations. She was somewhat chagrined to
admit that she only needed a third of what he'd printed
out, but she was certain that between Buck and
Nickelette, the rest would soon be spoken for. Nickelette,
too, immediately went to work, spending hours on
Pinterest gathering ideas for decorations, food, and
activities. Only Bill remained aloof, shaking his head
every time the party was mentioned. Penny hoped his
attitude wouldn't squelch the kids'—and her—
enthusiasm.

Penny had hoped the anticipation of her first-ever
birthday party would take her mind off the strange
backyard sighting, but the more she tried to forget it, the
more it occupied her thoughts. At times it seemed a
living thing that consciously sought her attention, so
much so that every clear night, she found herself drawn
outside to stare up at the sky. On those nights, she all but

rushed through supper so she could clear the table and make quick work of the dishes. She found herself uncharacteristically irritated if her family lingered around the table instead of going about their business immediately after eating.

If her family noticed her irritability or her increasingly-frequent ventures outside, they said nothing. Likewise, she said nothing to them—not even to her UFO-obsessed daughter—about her reasons for braving the chill of the Pennsylvania winter nights. Still, for all her diligent watchfulness, she saw nothing resembling her elusive mystery light, only the usual aircraft on their seemingly-endless paths across the sky.

One especially-frosty night in mid-February, Penny was again outside on the deck, staring up at the stars. In spite of her heavy winter coat, wool hat and scarf, and lined gloves, she shivered from the cold. She had just decided that maybe it was time to call it a night when the back door opened and Nickelette poked her head out. "Mom, are you out here?"

She turned slightly to face her daughter. "Yeah, baby. I'm over here."

Nickelette came outside wrapped in a blanket and padded over to Penny in her stocking feet. Leaning against her mother and enveloping her with the blanket, she asked, "What are you doing out here?"

"Just looking at the stars. And thinking." She brushed the hair back from her daughter's face. "Did you need something from me?"

"I just wanted to show you something I found for the party." She became animated as she took out her phone to pull up some pictures. "Look at these alien head pretzels and ET Rice Krispie treats."

Penny laughed. "Oh, they're adorable! We have to make those."

Nickelette kept scrolling. "And look at these UFOs. They're just crackers topped with cherry tomatoes, and green peppers for legs."

"I love it!" Penny had to admit, her daughter's enthusiasm was contagious. Nickelette was far more creative and outgoing than she had ever been, and she couldn't wait to see everything come together. "What are you planning for the cake?"

The glow from the phone made Nickelette's face appear ghostly as she grinned mischievously at her mother. "That's a surprise, but you're going to love it." She quickly shut down Pinterest and switched gears. "Can I order some stuff from Amazon? For the party?"

Penny raised an eyebrow. "I guess so, as long as you don't go overboard. We're not spending a fortune on this party."

"I won't. I just need some decorations and...stuff." She shut off her phone and turned to face Penny in the dark. "And no snooping. I want it to be a surprise."

Penny drew an X on her chest with a gloved finger. "Cross my heart and hope to fly."

At that moment, something in the sky caught their attention. Both women looked to a point above the horizon and immediately reacted.

"Mom! Is that a…"

"What is that?"

"It looks like…"

"It does look like…"

"Mom! It is! It's a UFO!"

Nickelette's squeals, coupled with Penny's exclamations soon drew the rest of the family. Buck dashed out the door with phone in hand and an ear bud in one ear. "What's happening?"

A moment later, Bill came storming out. "What's all the fuss out here? For God's sake, you'll wake the neighbors."

Penny spared her husband an irritated glance; she doubted any of the neighbors were actually sleeping at 8:23 on a Sunday night. Turning her attention back to the sky, she pointed to a slow-moving string of lights, which seemed to be growing brighter as they rose higher and higher in the night sky. "I think we've got a UFO."

"What? Oh, bull." He looked up at the lights and adjusted his glasses. After observing it for a moment, he said, "Huh."

"It's just Chinese lanterns or something, isn't it, Dad?" Buck asked, unimpressed.

"It is not, dork," Nickelette snapped, shooting him a dirty look as she aimed her phone skyward. "It's too high to be lanterns, and they're not flickering."

"Well, it's…" Unable to immediately come up with another plausible explanation, Buck put his hand to his ear, obviously straining to hear the person he was talking to. "Nickelette thinks there's a UFO. Go outside and look; you should be able to see it."

"I don't know," Bill said. "It's not lanterns; lanterns wouldn't travel in a perfectly straight line like that. It's not a plane, and it doesn't look like any satellite I've ever—whoa! Where'd they go?"

The entire family cried out at once as the lights suddenly vanished. "Tanner, did you see that?" Buck exclaimed, staring wide-eyed at the now-dark sky. "What the heck? What the actual heck?"

"I got it! I got it on my phone," Nickelette shouted, replaying the short video for Penny. "I actually got video of a UFO! Wait till my friends see this!"

"So did Tanner," Buck said. "He saw it too."

"Come on, it's not a UFO," Bill argued, though much less certain than before.

Buck turned to him. "Then what is it?"

"I don't know, but it's not a UFO. There's no such thing."

Nickelette finished watching the video for the third time and said to Buck, "We should call the news!"

"Yeah," Buck said. "We should."

"You're not calling the news." Bill was adamant. "Get that idea out of your heads right now."

"Well, I already posted it to Facebook and Instagram," Nickelette said, scrolling through her news feeds. "Hey, Buck, Tanner just posted his video to the news station's page."

"Oh, for Pete's sake. You people are making a big deal over what's probably nothing." Bill scanned the skies one last time. Seeing nothing impressive, he gave a dismissive wave. "Well, whatever it was, it's gone now. Let's get inside and get to bed. I have to work tomorrow, and you kids have school. You coming in, Penny?"

Penny, who had continued to stare silently up at the sky through their uproar, met her husband's gaze long enough to reply, "You go ahead. I'll be in after a bit."

Bill opened his mouth to say something, but then decided against it. Shaking his head in disgust, he pushed past Buck, who was standing in the doorway. Buck immediately followed him, still chatting excitedly with Tanner.

Despite her father's order, Nickelette remained outside with Penny, alternately looking down at her phone and then up at the sky, as if equally afraid of missing something either on social media or in the sky. "Do you think it'll come back?"

"I don't know," Penny responded, likewise staring up into the darkness. "I hope it does."

"Me too."

Penny and Nickelette kept up their cold, silent vigil for another half hour until clouds moved in and obscured most of the sky. The wind picked up and brought with it a blast of snow, just a few flakes at first, and then building into a squall. "Even if it does come back, we won't be able to see it," Nickelette said, briskly rubbing her arms against the chill. "I might as well go to bed."

She hurried inside, leaving Penny alone on the deck, still staring skyward as though expecting the UFO to reappear despite the heavy band of snow. It didn't take long for a layer of snow to cover her dark coat. Letting out a sigh, she brushed the snow from her coat and shook it from her hair. With one last glance at the sky, she went inside and locked the door.

Once inside, Penny paced around the living room, too wired to sleep. By the silence that pressed in around her, she guessed that her family hadn't been likewise affected by their close encounter. Still, hoping she might luck out and find someone awake, she crept back the hallway, stopping first at the room she shared with her husband. Not surprisingly, Bill was already snoring. Faint music came from Buck's room, a sign that he had indeed settled in for the night. Nickelette's room was dark and quiet, but Penny doubted she was sleeping. Not wanting to disturb either of them, she didn't knock on either door, but instead went back to the living room.

Settling in on the couch with an afghan, she picked up the remote and turned the TV on, quickly lowering the volume so as not to wake Bill. She flipped through the channels before stopping on one of the local stations that was airing the ten o'clock news. *Maybe they'll have something about the UFO*, she thought hopefully, laying the remote on her lap.

Penny sat with eyes glazed, staring at the screen,

but not really paying attention to the usual reports of crime, auto accidents, sports, and weather. Just as she was about to give up and turn the TV off, Damarys Nelson, the bright-eyed lead reporter smiled at the camera and announced, "We've received a number of reports of something strange in the skies over Dillsburg this evening. Here's Ryan Jacobs with more on this developing story. Ryan?"

With a gasp, Penny leaned forward so she wouldn't miss a single word of Ryan Jacobs' report, which turned out to be little more than a repeat of Damarys' words, enhanced by a couple viewer videos. One video included a zoomed-in shot of the lights, which didn't provide any clue as to what they might be, but it did emphasize the lights' strange progression across the sky before they disappeared.

When the report was finished, the camera returned to Damarys, who flashed an impossibly-white grin and said, "If anyone in our viewing area witnessed this UFO, we'd like to talk to you. Send us a message on our Facebook page, or call us at the number on the screen, and you might be featured on Channel 39 news. That's all for tonight. Thanks for watching, and join us tomorrow morning at 5:00 for Sunrise with Evan March."

As the closing credits scrolled, Penny's mind raced. She had seen the UFO, just as she'd seen the other one a few weeks ago, not to mention the ones she'd seen as a child. Maybe if she called the station and shared what she'd witnessed tonight, she could also talk about her other sightings. Maybe this time her experiences wouldn't be brushed off; maybe this time her experiences would be validated, and she could say for certain that there really was something more out there.

At breakfast the next morning, Penny sat bleary-eyed while her family consumed their usual assortment of cereal, toaster pastries, coffee, and juice, with bacon, hash browns, and a spinach and mushroom omelet for Bill. She almost thought her family had forgotten their close encounter from the previous night, until Nickelette glanced up from her phone to announce, "I got ninety-eight views and seventy-three likes on my UFO video. A bunch of other people said they saw it too."

Instantly awake, Penny sat up and said, "It was on Channel 39's news last night at ten, and on Channel 5's news at eleven. Someone even sent in a close-up shot."

"What the blazes were you doing up at that hour?" Bill asked, setting his coffee mug down with a thump. "No wonder you look like death warmed over."

"I couldn't sleep, so I turned the news on to see if they said anything about the UFO," Penny explained defensively. She took a long sip of her coffee. "Obviously they did. They want to interview someone who saw it."

Nickelette let out a gasp and set her phone down. As she opened her mouth to speak, Bill fixed his gaze on her and declared, "No, Nickelette, you are *not* doing an interview with the news. We've already given this UFO nonsense more time than it warrants."

In a rare fit of defiance, Penny glared at her husband and asked, "Why shouldn't one of us be interviewed? We saw the UFO just like all those other people did, and if the news thinks it's important—"

"Would you people stop with this UFO crap?" Bill threw his hands up in exasperation. "I told you last night it wasn't a UFO. There's a simple explanation for what we saw, and I guarantee someone will give that explanation in due time. I don't want to hear any more about it."

"But, Dad—"

"Give it up, Nickelette," Buck said, taking a third Pop Tart from the box. "It was cool to see, whatever it was, but I'm with Dad. That light wasn't a UFO any more than that hole in the yard a few years ago was the Bigfoot print you thought it was." He laughed at his clever retort.

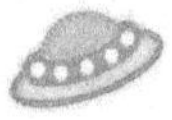

Sasha opened the pantry door and took out a wire basket filled with an assortment of single-serve coffee pods. Looking at Penny, she asked, "What would you like, Breakfast Blend or French Roast?"

Although Sasha always had at least half a dozen flavors on hand, she knew to only offer two of the more mundane choices to her friend, not because Penny disliked the flavored options, but because having too many options overwhelmed her. Some days, even choosing between two options was enough to make her anxious. However, today, the choice was an easy one to make. "French Roast. Please."

Raising an eyebrow, Sasha chuckled as she plucked a French Roast pod from the basket for Penny, and a Caramel Macchiato pod for herself. "French Roast, huh? Rough night?"

"I…didn't get much sleep last night."

"Mmm-hmm, I hear that." Sasha placed the French Roast pod into the machine and placed a New Orleans mug in place before hitting the *Brew* button. "One of the kids have a school assignment due today? Dharius pulled that one on me last week. Elias and I were up until three helping him put together a storyboard for an advertising project for his business ed. class."

Penny forced a laugh. "I remember that. How'd he make out?"

"He got a B- on it. Wasn't happy, but I told him he got better than he deserved after waiting till the last minute." Sasha removed Penny's mug and handed it to her before repeating the process with her Caramel Macchiato. "So which kid was it, and which class was it for?"

For a split second, she stared blankly at her friend, her foggy mind losing her train of thought. Finally, she made the connection. "It wasn't the kids, or even Bill. It was "—She hesitated. What would her friend think if she mentioned a UFO?—"I just couldn't sleep."

"The joys of middle age." Sasha brought her coffee and two dessert plates to the table and sat down. She gestured to the cake carrier sitting in front of Penny. "So what did you bring?"

Penny smiled as she removed the lid. "Sticky buns. With extra sticky and extra walnuts."

Sasha's eyes lit up, and she eagerly reached for one of the gooey pastries. Her eyes widened with delight as she savored the first bite. "Ooh, these are to die for! Did you make these?"

"No. Nickelette baked a double batch yesterday after school." She helped herself to a sticky bun and retrieved the walnut that fell off onto the table, popping it into her mouth. "I don't know why she did; Bill and Buck won't eat them. And heaven knows my hips don't need them."

"Those two don't know what's good." Sasha licked her fingers. "And these are good. Really good. That girl needs to open her own bakery."

Penny nodded her agreement. "She knows her way around the kitchen, that's for sure. You should see the menu she's got planned for the party."

"Girl, I can't believe you're having a birthday party." Sasha leaned forward, laughing as she slapped the table. "Was that Nickelette's idea?"

"No, it wasn't Nickelette's idea." Penny spoke more sharply than she intended; she softened her tone as she continued, "The theme was Nickelette's idea, but the party was mine. I told Bill I wanted something different this year."

Catching the slight edge in Penny's voice, Sasha studied her face for a moment and then gave her an encouraging smile. "Well, good for you, stepping out of your comfort zone and shaking things up. You need to show your family you're more than the mother ship that keeps the house running."

Penny started at her friend's choice of words, and she decided it was the perfect segue into the topic that still occupied her mind. "Speaking of mother ships, did you happen to see the news?"

Sasha cocked her head for a minute, thinking, until the light bulb came on. "Oh, you mean the UFO sighting?"

Penny could tell by her tone that she thought it was nonsense, but it was too late now; the subject had been broached. "Yeah."

She laughed. "Yeah, I heard about it this morning, but I didn't see anything."

Penny sipped her coffee, gauging Sasha's expression before venturing, "We saw it."

"For real?" Sasha drew back, obviously not sure what to think, then chuckled. "I'll bet Nickelette was in her glory."

"She was," Penny agreed. "It was pretty exciting."

Sasha shook her head, still not convinced. "It sounds to me like they had a slow news day."

"It really happened," Penny insisted. "Bill saw it too."

"Bill did?" If Penny's highly-analytical husband had seen it, Sasha was more inclined to listen. "What did he say?"

"He said he didn't know what it was," Penny said, drawing herself up just a bit taller, feeling important because she'd been allowed to witness such a great mystery. "He said he's never seen such a thing. Of course, he still brushed it off as something that could be rationally explained."

"Huh." Sasha gave her a blank stare, for the moment unable to refute the experience. At last, she gave her head a shake and broke off a piece of sticky bun. "Well, I'm with Bill on that. You know I don't put any stock in UFOs."

Penny's shoulders sagged, feeling a loss of support. What would her friend say if she knew— "That wasn't the first time I've seen a UFO."

"Say what?" Her eyes snapped up to meet Penny's. "For real? You ain't pulling my leg, now. When was this?"

Penny took another walnut from her sticky bun and put it in her mouth, chewing longer than she needed to, suddenly wishing she hadn't spoken so rashly. She swallowed and looked up at Sasha. "A couple weeks ago. I was out on the deck late, after everyone else went inside, and...I saw a UFO."

"Well, what did it look like?"

"At first it was just a bright light in the sky. I thought it was just a plane." Now that she had begun telling about her experience, the words just spilled out of her mouth as she related how the light had intensified until it was almost blinding. "Then this beam of brighter white light came down and surrounded me, and I heard a voice inviting me to come with them."

Sasha had leaned forward, hanging on her friend's every word. When Penny stopped speaking, the spell was broken, and Sasha gave her head a shake and joked, "Girl, are you sure you weren't channeling Styx?" She sang a few bars of "Come Sail Away" before the wounded expression on Penny's face silenced her. "I'm sorry, Penny. Obviously you didn't go with them, so what happened?"

Penny hesitated, reluctant to say more after Sasha's disbelieving reaction to what she had already shared. Still, she felt that she needed to tell someone about her experience. "That's pretty much all there is to it. Before I could either agree to go with them or tell them 'no thanks,' Bill came back outside—"

"Did Bill see it?"

"He did, actually," Penny responded, glad that someone else had seen the strange light, even if he had interpreted it differently. "But all he saw was the light shooting off into the sky and disappearing. He thought it was just a meteorite, or as he called it, a fireball."

"Huh." Sasha's eyebrows drew together as she held Penny's gaze, and Penny was certain that she agreed with Bill's assessment. After a moment, she said, "But you know it wasn't."

Penny's hands tightened around her mug. She wished she could make her friend believe, but she knew that was impossible. "Look, I don't have a degree in science, but I know what I saw. It wasn't a plane, it wasn't a meteorite, it wasn't a Chinese lantern. It was…something else." She held her friend's gaze, silently pleading with her to understand. "Do you think I'm crazy?"

For a long, uncomfortable moment, Sasha said nothing. She wanted to believe Penny, but she just couldn't wrap her mind around what her friend claimed had happened. "No, of course, I don't think you're crazy."

"But you don't believe I saw a UFO."

Sasha swirled the remains of her coffee in her mug as she considered her words. "Penny, I believe you saw something, but a spaceship? Little green men?"

Penny threw her hands up in frustration. "For heaven's sake, Sasha, I never said anything about little green men."

"I'm sorry. I just—"

"Come on, Sasha. Go outside some night and look up at the stars. Can you tell me that you really believe that in all those billions of stars there's not another planet that has some form of life?"

Sasha said nothing, but simply studied the earnestness in Penny's eyes; she was rarely so animated or so adamant. A chill ran down her back as she understood that *something* had happened to her friend.

The sound of the front door opening and closing announced Bill's return from work, but Penny didn't budge from the couch. Her eyes were glued to the TV, which was tuned to the 6:00 news. She wasn't interested in the reports of a fire at a local restaurant, or the arrest of three people on drug charges, or the interview with a congressman visiting the area. She only wanted to see the story announced at the beginning of the newscast, the follow-up on the previous night's UFO story, with commentary from an as-yet-unnamed expert.

Penny heard Bill set down his briefcase, remove his overcoat, and hang it in the closet. She heard his heavy footsteps come up the stairs and pause. Out of the corner of her eye, she saw him peer into the dark kitchen and then into the dining room where the table sat devoid of plates and silverware. She felt a twinge of guilt; perhaps she should have set the table, or at least asked Nickelette to do it, before sitting down in front of the TV. *Oh, never mind,* she thought. *It'll only take a minute to do it when this is over.*

Bill took a couple steps into the living room and looked first at Penny, then at the television, and then back to Penny. "What's going on here? Why isn't supper ready?"

Penny turned her attention away from the TV long enough to inform her husband, "There's a casserole in the oven. There's something on the news I want to see; I'll have supper on the table as soon as this is over."

"Well, that's a fine how-do-you-do. A man comes home after working overtime and—"

"Here it is!" Penny half-rose from her seat to call to her daughter. "Nickelette! The UFO story is on!"

Nickelette's bedroom door opened, and she dashed down the hallway and into the living room, almost plowing into Bill as she passed. She sat down next to Penny and asked, "Did I miss anything?"

"Not yet. They're just rehashing what they reported last night. They have an expert coming on to weigh in."

"Who's the expert?" Nickelette asked.

Buck had sauntered out of his room and stood next to Bill. Hearing his sister's question, he raked his hands through his hair to make it stand up wildly. "Probably Giorgio Tsoukalos. I'm not saying it was aliens, but…aliens."

Bill laughed at his son's impression, but Penny and Nickelette shot him dirty looks before turning their attention back to the TV. At that moment, the evening newscaster, Jose Rodriguez, introduced the promised expert. "Joining us live from West Virginia is Dr. Alexander Rokuskie, Professor of Astrophysics at Eberley University. Dr. Rokuskie, thank you for joining us this evening."

"Eberley University? Where the blazes is that?" Bill said. "They couldn't get someone from Penn State or

Messiah; they had to go to Hickville?"

Buck snorted. "Well, they probably had to search high and low for someone who's an expert in that UFOlogy crap."

"Shh!" Penny glared at them as she turned the volume up. "I want to hear this."

Jose Rodriguez had cut to a clip of one of the viewer-submitted videos. "Dr. Rokuskie, we had no fewer than a dozen videos sent to us showing this phenomenon last night. This one was sent in by Lynette Strayer from York. Can you shed a little light on what we're seeing here?"

There was a moment of silence as the string of lights moved across the screen and then disappeared one by one. After the last light had winked out of sight, the camera cut to a split screen showing both the newscaster and the professor. Dr. Rokuskie removed his thick, dark-framed glasses and looked into the camera. "That's a quality bit of footage," he said, giving a curt nod. "I'm impressed with the clarity of the video. Kudos to you, Ms. Strayer. Jose, you say this was visible throughout your viewing area?"

"Yes, it was," Jose said, fidgeting as though trying to contain his excitement and retain a professional air. "And we had reports that folks outside the viewing area could see it as well. Clearly, what our viewers want to know is, what are we looking at here? Is this an attempt at extraterrestrial contact—or even invasion—or is there a more mundane explanation?"

Dr. Rokuskie laughed. "Well, Jose, I can assure you that this isn't a 3-D, real-life game of Asteroids in the making, even though it may look that way from the video clip. What we're looking at here is what's called a StarTrain link-up. StarTrain is the first wave of what will eventually become a constellation, or group, of approximately twelve thousand small, mass-produced satellites—"

"Wait, what?" Jose's eyes bulged as his jaw dropped in disbelief. "Twelve *thousand*? What are all those satellites for?"

"For the most part," Dr. Rokuskie explained, "their intended purpose is to enable worldwide satellite internet access, but some of those satellites will be used for military and scientific purposes, and for exploration…"

Penny had heard enough. She turned off the TV and sat staring at the dark screen for a moment before exchanging a crestfallen look with Nickelette. So there hadn't been a UFO after all.

As if the women hadn't already grasped the truth of the previous night's sighting, Bill laughed loudly at the grand joke on his wife and daughter. "See, Penny? I told you there was a logical explanation. Like I said, there's no such thing as UFOs."

"Of course, Bill," Penny said dejectedly. "You were right. You always are." Although she didn't believe the words she forced from her lips, she didn't have it in her at that moment to disagree with him, to give a voice to what she still believed to be true.

Satisfied by his wife's acquiescence, Bill gave a curt nod. "Good. Now that this nonsense is settled, how about you get supper on the table?"

Nickelette got to her feet and plodded off in the direction of the hallway, head hung low and shoulders slumped. "I don't want any supper," she said. "I'm not hungry."

Buck laughed, heedless of her disappointment. "All full up on humble pie, are you, Nickelette? Now you'll have to post on Instagram that you got punked by SpaceX."

"Shut up, Buck," she mumbled before going to her room and shutting the door.

Penny was already in her pajamas and under the covers when Bill came back the hall to get ready for bed later that night. She listened to him going through his nightly routine: shower, blow-dry what hair he had left, wash his face at the sink, brush his teeth…every night going through the same motions, every night taking twenty-seven minutes. When he finally flushed the toilet and emerged from the bathroom, she rolled over onto her side, facing the window, hoping he would think she was asleep. No such luck.

He slipped into bed and said, "The dirty dishes are still in the sink. Don't you usually wash them right after supper?"

Too numb to be very much annoyed at his comment, she assured him, "I'll do them in the morning."

"Well, I don't want to wake up to ants in the kitchen."

For real? You're worried about ants? "It's the middle of February, Bill. We're not going to get ants in the kitchen."

Much to Penny's surprise, it seemed that Bill actually heard the flat tone of her voice. "Are you still upset over that UFO nonsense?"

What do you care? Penny thought, the memory of his mocking comments stinging her pride all over again. Not wanting to dredge up the conversation, she lied, "No."

"I should hope not." He punched his pillow four times before settling down. "It's not worth making such a fuss over."

"If you say so."

Bill turned to face her, but seeing only the back of her head, he raised himself up on one elbow. "Come on, Pen. What's going on? I can understand Nickelette acting like a kid who just found out Santa Claus isn't real, but you?"

Penny let out a huff and rolled over onto her back to stare at the ceiling. "Just forget it, Bill. You wouldn't understand."

"So explain it to me." He lifted his hand and let it

fall onto the comforter. "Make me understand."

By the tone of his voice, Penny guessed he truly had little interest in trying to understand, but she figured if he were going to make even a half-hearted attempt at hearing her out, then she was going to meet him halfway. "When we're outside looking up at the stars, watching for meteorites, don't you ever wonder if there's something else out there?"

"No."

Penny turned her head slightly, just so she could see her husband. "Not ever?"

"No, never." Clearly, Penny had underestimated the limitations of his worldview. "Look, I've never read or heard any evidence that was enough to convince me otherwise. This is the only planet that has intelligent life. Or any life, for that matter."

Penny's heart sank. She knew it was futile trying to make him see the world from her eyes, but she pressed on, wanting, needing to find even the smallest bit of common ground. "But don't you ever wish there was something more out there?"

"Now why in the world would I wish something like that?" He lay down again, already growing tired of the conversation.

"I don't know," Penny muttered. "It's just that sometimes the world...my world just seems...small. I want there to be something more."

"What do you mean you want something more?" Bill sat up and looked pointedly at his wife. "For God's sake, Penny, I've given you a house, a car, the kids. I don't make you go out and get a job. I let you have lunch with your friends. I'm letting you have this Area 51 birthday party. You've got a good life, Penny. What more do you need?"

Tears stung her eyes, but she refused to let them fall. He just didn't understand, and she couldn't make him understand. As she had done so many times before, she withdrew into herself, cursing herself for daring to open up to him, "I guess I didn't think of that," she said. "You're right. I should be thankful for everything you've provided."

"That's my girl." He leaned over to kiss her. "You and Nickelette need to focus on your big party; that's only a couple weeks away, you know."

"I know."

Bill lay down again and pulled the covers up to his chin. "Good night, Penny. I love you."

"Good night, Bill. I love you too."

Within minutes, Bill was snoring, but Penny lay awake, still mulling over their conversation as silent tears spilled from her eyes and trickled down her temples to pool in her ears. It wasn't Bill's lack of belief in UFOs that upset her so; it was his unwillingness to accept the existence of anything outside of his realm of experience.

At last, unable to sleep, or to even silence her mind, Penny slipped out of bed and went to the window. She parted the curtains and leaned her elbows on the windowsill to peer out at the star-filled night. A single jet crossed the sky and disappeared over the mountain. "I know there's something more out there," she whispered. "I just know there is."

In the days leading up to her party, Penny said nothing more about the UFO, either to Bill or to anyone else, but that didn't mean she'd put it out of her mind. Even as she threw herself into party preparations with Nickelette, she still thought about the UFO, not the one that Dr. Rokuskie had debunked on the news, but the *real* one, the one she'd seen weeks before, as well as the one she'd seen as a child. The more she thought about it, the more she grew certain that the two UFOs were one and the same, and that she would see it again someday.

One day a few days before the party, as she helped Nickelette cut out poster board spaceships and stencil lime green aliens on a black paper border, Penny almost told her about the other UFO, the real UFO. She knew her daughter would understand, and more importantly, would believe her. However, just as she opened her mouth to share her experience, a sudden thought made her stop. What if Nickelette *did* believe her? What if her belief was so strong that she, too, took to scanning the night skies in hopes of seeing her mother's UFO? And what if she *did* see the UFO, and what if she, too, was invited to come aboard? That was the thought that chilled Penny to the bone. Nickelette was much more adventurous than Penny was, and there was no doubt in Penny's mind that if given the chance, Nickelette would, without hesitation, hop aboard a spaceship and see where it took her. The very idea that her daughter would board the UFO and leave her behind filled Penny with terror. As her gaze rested on her daughter, busily designing props for a photo booth, Penny decided to keep her UFO encounter to herself, guarding it as she would a treasure, or a secret.

"You would have to pick the coldest night of the year for your party," Bill grumbled, reaching down to turn the heat up full blast as he shot Penny a look of irritation as though she had indeed planned the weather for this night.

"Not my fault," she quipped, barely sparing her husband a glance. "You can blame Punxatawney Phil. He's the one who forecast an early spring."

Bill muttered something under his breath, but Penny paid him no mind. She was going to enjoy this evening, even if it was only fifteen degrees outside. The hopelessness and low spirits that had plagued her over the past couple weeks had finally lifted. She had awakened that morning with a sense of excitement and anticipation, sensing that somehow today, her birthday, was a new beginning. She was determined to use this party as a springboard to break out of her self-imposed Area 51, as Buck continued to call her introversion, and become a new Penny Dimeler. No, Bill wasn't going to spoil her evening, no matter how grumpy he was.

When they pulled into the church parking lot a minute later, Bill immediately hit the brakes and stared. Buck and Nickelette had been at the church for most of the day, decorating and getting the food ready. By the looks of things, they had outdone themselves. Multi-colored lights pulsated through the translucent windows of the social hall, and around the dormant flower garden next to the handicapped entrance, bright yellow *Police Line Do Not Cross* tape marked off an elaborate UFO crash scene. Penny laughed as she admired the fluorescent blue disc outlined with fairy lights that sat at an angle in the snow, as well as the deflated balloon alien "victims" lying near the wreckage.

Bill leaned over for a closer look and then barked out, "Is that my trash can lid? It is! It is my trash can lid! No wonder I couldn't find it. They'd better hope that paint comes off, or I'll have their—"

"I think it's clever," Penny interrupted, turning to glare at him. "You should be glad I wouldn't let them buy the party prop they found online for $150." Bill's jaw dropped in outrage, but before he could spew a single word, Penny cut him off. "I said they didn't buy it, so just forget about it."

Still grumbling under his breath about the foolishness of a party for a middle-aged woman, Bill maneuvered the car into a space between Buck's well-used Ford Focus and a pickup truck hitched to a small trailer emblazoned with DJ Diz-E Daggz. He turned off the ignition and turned to Penny, still looking for a reason to complain. "A DJ? They hired a DJ? How much did that set us back?"

"The DJ is one of Buck's friends from school," Penny said wearily, removing her seat belt. "Buck helped him fix his truck in exchange for tonight." She opened the door and got out before Bill could find another nit to pick.

Penny made her way up the steps without waiting for Bill. Just as she made it to the entrance, which held a sign that read "Area 51: Do Not Enter," Bill came trotting up the steps and reached around her to open the door for her. "For Pete's sake, Penny, what's your rush? You could have waited for me."

She breezed past him into the entryway and was about to respond when two young men wearing black suits and sunglasses stepped out of the shadows. One held out a red light saber to block her way, and the other held up a flashlight covered with blue cellophane and shined it into her face. "Ah, yes," he said, gesturing to his partner to let her pass. "The guest of honor. You may proceed, but speak to no one about our encounter."

Startled at first, Penny gasped and took a step back; then, recognizing the Men in Black as Buck and his friend Kenny, she chuckled and started down the narrow hallway toward the social hall.

Bill didn't find their actions quite as amusing. When Buck shined the flashlight in his face, Bill smacked it away. "Knock it off, Buck. I know that's you in that get-up. I hope you're not planning to harass everyone who comes in."

Refusing to break character, Buck replied in a flat voice, "This is Area 51. Access is granted only to authorized individuals."

"Well, I paid to rent this place," Bill said, pushing past them to follow Penny. "That makes me authorized personnel."

Penny turned to shake her head at him. He seemed as determined to have a miserable time as she was to have a good time. "Honestly, Bill, let the kids have their fun. They're not hurting anything."

Undaunted by Bill's attitude, the Men in Black choked back their laughter as they retreated back to their respective corners to await their next victims.

Nickelette was waiting by the door as Penny entered the social hall. She thrust a neon green gift bag into her mother's hands and gushed, "Quick, Mom. You have to open this before the other guests get here."

Slightly taken aback, Penny hesitated. "What? Why? Don't you want me to wait until I open the other gifts?"

"No, you have to open it now," she repeated. "You have to wear this for the party."

Bill overheard the exchange as he came in behind Penny. "Criminy, Nickelette. At least let your mother take her coat off."

Still barely able to contain her excitement, Nickelette held the gift bag while Bill helped Penny with her coat. As he hung up his coat and Penny's on the rack by the door, Penny took the gift bag and reached inside. She drew out an article of clothing wrapped in white tissue paper. Setting the empty gift bag on the floor at her feet, she unfolded the bundle and laughed. It was indeed a black T-shirt, obviously designed by Nickelette. On the front, in neon fabric paint, were the silhouettes of an alien and a woman dancing in the light beam from a hovering UFO. Beneath the graphic were the words, "Welcome to Area 51."

Penny's breath caught in her throat as the painted image once more brought to mind the real UFO she still hoped to see again. Even as she stared at the image on the shirt, in her mind she could hear a voice saying, *"Penny…Penny, are you ready? Are you coming?"*

"Mom? Mom, what's wrong?" Penny became aware of Nickelette speaking to her. She glanced up into her daughter's anxious eyes. "Don't you like it? Buck and I made it for you."

Quickly pasting a smile on her face, Penny responded, "Of course! I love it! I was just…surprised. This is amazing!"

Relief flooded Nickelette's face as she hurried over to the light switch. "And that's not all. Watch this." She turned the overhead lights off and flipped another switch, which turned on half a dozen black light bars mounted on the ceiling. "Look at how it glows."

Penny held up the shirt in the purplish glow. She laughed, delighted at the way the design lit up. "Nickelette, this is…what do you kids say…epic. You outdid yourself this time."

"That's the understatement of the year," Bill muttered.

Penny turned to look at him. He wasn't looking at the T-shirt, but rather was taking in the social hall, now aglow with neon aliens, spaceships, stars, and planets. Even some of the items on the food table glowed eerily under the black lights. Grinning broadly, she turned again to Nickelette. "You really did outdo yourself. This is going to be a night to remember."

An hour later, the party was in full swing. To Bill's chagrin and Penny's surprise, everyone on the guest list had come out to celebrate her birthday. She couldn't help smiling as she looked around at the friends and family seated around every one of the tables Buck and Nickelette had set up.

Still, while Penny was delighted that so many had come to her last-minute party, she had to admit that she was exhausted and overwhelmed. She had already made the rounds to all the adult guests, making small talk and thanking them for coming. Now as she sat at a table with

Sasha, Betty, and her sister-in-law LaDonna, listening to them recount their latest NetFlix binges, she realized that she had underestimated how draining all the mingling would be. As she nibbled on a plateful of UFO crackers and tried to be attentive enough to respond appropriately to questions and comments, in her mind, she was wishing she were at home on her deck, scanning the skies for the one thing that would truly make her birthday complete.

All of a sudden, the music went silent, and the black lights went out, plunging the entire social hall into darkness, save for the strings of green alien-head lights around the doorways and gift table, and the UFO-themed luminaria on each of the tables. After a moment, "2001: A Space Odyssey" began blaring from the sound system, and the swinging door to the kitchen opened. Amid gasps and exclamations of surprise, Nickelette came out carrying a cake alit with candles. The guests applauded as she brought the cake to Penny's table and set it down in front of her.

Penny let out an exclamation of delight as she admired the simple but clever design. The sheet cake was frosted green to resemble a field. Plastic cows were scattered about, and a small hand-lettered sign that read "Welcome to Area 51" had been placed in one corner. In the very center of the cake stood an inverted clear plastic cup with a plastic cow suspended inside it. Balanced on top of the cup was a small, saucer-shaped cake, frosted blue and decorated with candy to resemble a spaceship.

A ring of birthday candles glowed around its edges. As the guests gathered around to take pictures, Sasha began to sing "Happy Birthday," and everyone joined in.

When the song ended, Penny sat staring delightedly at the cake, until Buck said, "Make a wish and blow out the candles, Mom!"

"Oh!" Penny felt silly for having forgotten what to do, but she assured herself, *It's not as though I've had a lot of birthday parties.* It only took a moment to make her wish, and then she took a deep breath and blew out all the candles.

As guests alternately clapped and fanned away the smoke, Bill and Penny's niece Naomi piped up, "What did you wish for, Aunt Penny?"

"Whoa, whoa, whoa! She can't tell her wish," Dharius said. "If she does, it won't come true."

"That's right, sweetheart," Penny said laying her hand on Naomi's cheek. "It has to be a secret wish so it comes true."

Bill barked out a laugh. "If you wished for an army of little green men to jump out of the cake, that won't come true anyway." A few people laughed at his joke, encouraging him to comment further. "I'm used to my daughter's obsession with extraterrestrials, but after my wife had an emotional breakdown over the StarTrain satellites, I was afraid it was becoming contagious."

The good-natured laughter that had broken out over Bill's initial joke dwindled to nervous titters, and for a long, uncomfortable moment, no one knew what to say.

Penny stared at her husband, her heart pierced by the betrayal she felt over his making such a comment in front of their friends and relatives. A glance at Nickelette told her that she, too, was mortified over being called out. Fortunately, at that moment, Naomi, who was blissfully unaware of the tension, again spoke up. "Aunt Penny, isn't it time to open presents? I want you to open mine first."

Penny swallowed hard and smiled too broadly. "You're right, Naomi. I'll open my presents, and then we'll have cake and ice cream."

Sasha and Nickelette took over the task of cutting the cake and scooping the ice cream while Penny started on the small pile of cards and gifts that Naomi handed her one by one. As she smiled and laughed and admired each offering, she played the part of a woman who was having a marvelous time with family and friends, but inside she was shattered.

Each time she laid a gift card, a book, a scarf, or an alien-themed trinket on the table next to her, she glanced at Bill, who was now laughing and chatting with his friends and paying no attention to her. She marveled over the growing realization that the man who should be closer to her than anyone else now seemed more of an alien to her than the beings who had beckoned to her from the strange light in the sky.

A little while later, Penny set aside her half-eaten plate of cake and ice cream. The cake was delicious—a mocha-hazelnut confection that Nickelette had come up with herself—but it stuck in her throat like a rock, and not even her favorite pistachio ice cream would help it go down. Bill's insensitive jabs continued to play through her mind, dragging her deflated mood further and further down.

She let out a sigh and allowed her gaze to travel around the room. Buck, Kenny, and some of his other friends were dancing to "Men in Black." Nickelette and her friends were taking selfies at the photo booth. Bill was sitting at a table with Sasha, Elias, and his work friends. Others were chatting or helping themselves to more snacks or drinks. By the looks of things, everyone was having a great time.

Everyone but Penny.

Penny sighed again and quietly slipped out of the social hall, down the hallway, and out the door to stand on the stairs by the entrance. The "Area 51" sign now hung askew and flapped forlornly in the cold wind that had begun blowing.

Turning away from the door, she noticed right away that the parking lot seemed to be unusually dark. Looking around, she realized that the streetlight on the corner by the church wasn't lit, and neither was the light over the entrance. *That's odd,* she thought, wondering if she should go inside and inform someone. In the end, she decided not to. She actually preferred the darkness.

Leaning against the railing, Penny looked up at the sky. The almost-full moon had barely cleared the horizon, so the stars were still fully visible. She breathed in the icy air and smiled as her heavy heart began to lift. Scanning the sky, she found first the Big Dipper, and then Orion. "Hello there, Orion," she said, dipping her head to acknowledge him. "Today is my birthday." She imagined that the constellation twinkled even brighter as if in response.

As she continued to gaze upward, a light appeared just over the mountain, most likely a jet on approach to Harrisburg. Penny watched the light for a moment, for once not caring who was on board or where they were headed.

A shout of laughter from inside drew Penny's attention, and she looked toward the windows where the colored lights still pulsated. She felt a slight twinge in her chest as she wondered if Bill was making wisecracks about her again. She lowered her gaze to her clasped hands. In the dim light shining through the glass doors from the hallway, she studied her chipped purple nail polish and twirled her wedding and engagement rings around on her finger. She knew she should go back inside—it was her party, after all—but it occurred to her that she was actually more content out here alone in the cold than she would be inside surrounded by family and friends.

As that knowledge sank in, she turned her attention back to the skies. Her eyes widened in shock as she realized that the jet was now directly overhead, but it was no longer moving. Penny got the impression that the light was watching her, and had been doing so for several minutes. No sooner had she reached that conclusion than the light began to grow larger and brighter. Within seconds, it grew so large that Penny was certain she could reach out and touch it.

A beam of silver-white light descended from the bright light, but this time it didn't envelop her. Instead, the column of light reached down to the ground at the bottom of the stairs. As she stared at the circle of light shimmering on the macadam only a couple yards away, she heard again the familiar voice calling to her. *"Penny…Penny, come with us. Are you coming? Penny…Penny…"*

Her mind began to swim as she wrestled once again with the choice set before her. In her mind's eye, she saw the faces of her loved ones: Bill. Buck and Nickelette. Naomi. Sasha. She thought about her house, her church, her hometown, all the places she loved to go…

"Come with us," the voice entreated, and Penny sensed that they understood the reasons for her indecision. *"Come and see the stars up close. Explore the Milky Way. See wonders you've never imagined. Come with us, Penny. Come with us…"*

Suddenly, the door behind her swung open. "Hey, Mom. Are you…oh my word! *Mom!*"

Looking over her shoulder, Penny saw Nickelette

standing in the doorway, staring wide-eyed and slack-jawed at the blinding light hovering barely a hundred feet above. As she realized what was happening, she turned and ran back inside, shouting, "Dad! Buck! Everyone! Come quick! It's a UFO, a *real* UFO!"

"*Penny...*"

As Nickelette's voice continued to echo from inside, Penny turned her attention back to the light. As her eyes adjusted to the brightness, for the first time she was able to make out the outline of a metallic, saucer-shaped craft that seemed to be spinning. Although she saw no windows, she knew that whoever—or whatever—controlled the craft could see her.

"*Are you coming, Penny?*"

She lowered her gaze once more to the shimmering beam that descended from the craft, and her trepidation began to melt away. Taking a deep breath, she took one hesitant step toward it, and then another. Still, she wasn't sure. Part of her wanted to board the craft and soar away into the heavens, but another part of her resisted. What about—

The door to the church crashed open, and Nickelette stumbled through, grabbing the railing at the top of the steps to keep herself from tumbling down. "Mom! Mom, what are you doing?"

With one hand on the railing, Penny turned and looked up at her daughter as Buck and Kenny came to the door and stopped, gaping. "What the..." Buck exclaimed. "That's not possible!"

"I can't believe it," Kenny said, removing his sunglasses to squint at the light, and then putting them back on to block the intensity.

"What is going on out here?" Bill's voice rang out from inside. "Haven't we had enough of this UFO nonsense?" He reached the door and shoved past Buck and Kenny to step out onto the walkway. "Penny, you need to get hold of yourself and—*what the blazes?*"

Penny watched Bill's face blanch at the reality of the unbelievable situation playing out before him. She smiled with satisfaction, seeing every shred of her husband's self-important skepticism shatter and fall all around him. "Still think there's nothing else out there, Bill?"

As Bill's terror-stricken gaze shifted from the whirling, glowing spaceship to his smirking wife, he tried unsuccessfully to dismiss what he was seeing. "This isn't...you don't expect me to...Penny, this is just...just one of the kids' tricks."

Penny barked out a laugh and turned again toward the shimmering beam of light in front of her. This time there was no hesitation as she started boldly toward it.

Just outside the beam, she stopped and looked up. Several silhouettes peered from an opening at the bottom of the craft, next to the place from which the beam of light emanated. One of the beings appeared to lean over and wave at her. The last remnant of her fear vanished, and she extended her hand into the beam. The light was warm, and it made her skin feel fizzy, as though she'd plunged her hand into a glass of soda. At the same time, she watched as her hand pixilated before her eyes, and she drew back quickly.

"Do not be afraid." A voice spoke into her mind. *"You will not be harmed."*

She swallowed hard and was about to step into the shimmering beam when a brief commotion erupted behind her, followed by a plaintive voice calling, "Mom?"

Penny turned again to see Nickelette, halfway down the steps, with Bill tugging at her arm, trying to hold her back. She saw reflected in her daughter's face the same wanderlust tinged with fear that she had felt for so long. As she watched Nickelette struggling to break free from Bill's grasp, something inside her snapped. With a surge of defiance, she caught Bill's eye and said sharply, "Bill, you let her go! You've held me back for years; I won't let you hold Nickelette back too!"

Bill was so taken aback by his usually-docile wife's aggressive tone that he loosened his grip on his daughter as he returned Penny's steely gaze. "What! What do you mean I've held you back? After all I've given you, this is the—*Nickelette!* You get back here, young lady!"

Taking advantage of her father's distraction, Nickelette broke free and rushed down the steps toward her mother, while keeping a wary eye on the craft above.

Penny reached for her daughter's hand and said,

"Come on, girl. This is what you've been wishing for. We're going on an adventure."

For the briefest moment, Nickelette's eyes widened in fear, and Penny thought she might refuse. Then she joined her mother, and together they stepped into the shimmering beam.

As they slowly rose toward the hovering spacecraft, Penny gazed down at her family and the friends who had come outside to see what was happening. Sasha stood in the doorway with eyes like saucers and a wonder-filled smile on her face. Bill still stood in the same spot, clutching the railing and yelling, "Penny! Penny, you come back here! You can't leave me! Who's going to make dinner? Who's going to pack my lunch? Penny!"

When the two women were inside the craft, the door on the bottom slid shut, the beam of light vanished, and the spacecraft shot off into the night, leaving behind a small crowd of shocked spectators.

THE END

ABOUT THE AUTHOR

L. P. Hawk is a writer and independently-published author of the *Kyrie Carter: Supernatural Sleuth* paranormal mystery series. A lifelong storyteller, she often uses writing as a way to explore the questions, insecurities, and great mysteries of life that never seem to be far from her wandering mind. As a substitute teacher and stay-at-home mother to two teenagers and a dog, she has seen and heard weirdness that rivals anything she has ever written in her books.

www.ingramcontent.com/pod-product-compliance
Lightning Source LLC
Chambersburg PA
CBHW071443150726
48000CB00006B/2425